LITTLE MISS NEAT

by Roger Hargreaves

EGMONT

Little Miss Neat was a very tidy person.

Probably the tidiest person in the world.

She lived in Twopin Cottage.

It was called Twopin Cottage because she kept
it as neat as two pins!

She just couldn't stand a mess.

Every day she spent all day polishing and dusting
and cleaning and making sure that things were in
their proper places.

One morning Little Miss Neat awoke in her bedroom at Twopin Cottage.

She looked out of her bedroom window.

It had been raining during the night, and there was a puddle in the middle of her garden path.

"Oh!" she gasped in horror, and rushed outside with a duster.

She mopped up every drop of puddle, and then she rushed inside and washed the duster, and then she ironed the duster, and then she folded the duster, and then she placed the duster very neatly back in its drawer.

Everything in Twopin Cottage had its proper place!

Now, this story is about the time Little Miss Neat went on holiday.

She always went away for one week every summer, and this year was no different.

She spent two weeks packing.

And then she spent a whole day polishing her suitcase.

And then off she set, leaving Twopin Cottage all spick and span and neat and tidy.

"Oh, I hope it doesn't get too dusty while I'm away," she thought as she closed the door behind her.

But something worse than dusty was going to happen to Twopin Cottage.

Would you like to know what?

Mr Muddle came to tea!

He'd written to Miss Neat to tell her, but, being Mr Muddle, he somehow got into a muddle posting the letter.

Actually, what happened was that when Mr Muddle went to post the letter he had the letter in one hand and a half-eaten sandwich in the other.

And you can guess what happened, can't you?

That's right!

He posted the sandwich!

A posted cheese sandwich!

"It'll be nice seeing Miss Neat again," he chuckled to himself as he walked home.

"This sandwich is a bit chewy," he thought.

It was the day after Miss Neat left that Mr Muddle arrived.

He walked up the garden path of Twopin Cottage, and knocked at the door.

No reply!

"Goodbye!" he shouted.

It should have been "Hello!" but he isn't called Mr Muddle for nothing.

"Nobody home?" he called.

He pushed open the door.

"Oh dear," he thought as he looked around.

"Nobody home!"

"Never mind," he thought. "I'll make myself a cup of tea and wait for Miss Neat."

So he went into the kitchen of Twopin Cottage, made himself a cup of tea, and waited.

And waited.

And waited.

And waited.

And went home.

Little Miss Neat stepped out of the taxi outside Twopin Cottage.

"That was a lovely holiday," she said, paying the taxi driver. "But it's nice to be home."

She walked up the garden path, and went in through the door.

"Not too dusty," she said to herself, looking around.

"I think I'll make myself a nice cup of tea before
I start unpacking."

But, making tea after a Mr Muddle visit isn't quite
as easy as it sounds.

Little Miss Neat eventually found the teapot.

Not in its proper place.

In the refrigerator!

And she eventually found the milk.

Not in its proper place.

In the teapot!

And the tea. In the sugar bowl!

And the sugar. In the milk jug!

And a cup. In the oven!

And a saucer. In the bread bin!

But, could she find a teaspoon?

She could not!

The telephone rang. Little Miss Neat picked it up.

"Hello," she said.

At the other end of the line Mr Muddle suddenly realised he was holding the telephone the wrong way round.

He turned it the right way round.

"Goodbye," he said.

"Who's that?" asked Miss Neat.

"It's you," replied Mr Muddle.

Miss Neat thought.

"It's Mr Muddle, isn't it?" she guessed.

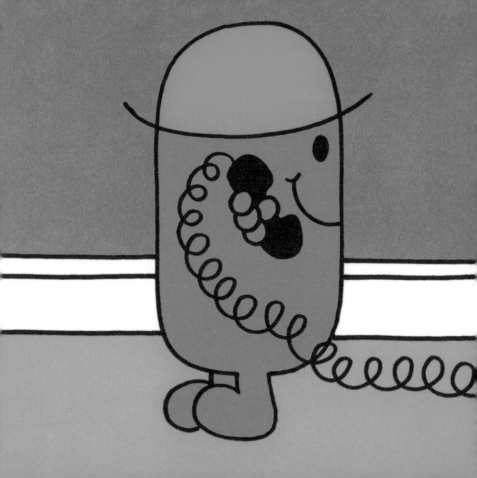

"Yes," replied Mr Muddle, getting it right for once.

"And you paid me a visit while I was away on holiday, didn't you?" she guessed again.

"Yes," replied Mr Muddle, getting it right for twice.

"Can I come and see you now you're back?"

"I suppose so," sighed Miss Neat.

"Goodbye!"

"Hello!" said Mr Muddle.

And put the phone down.

Little Miss Neat sighed a heavy sigh, and sat down in the armchair next to the telephone.

Ouch!!

She looked underneath the cushion.

There were all her teaspoons.

And knives!

And forks!

I don't think Little Miss Neat will be taking a holiday next year.

Do you?